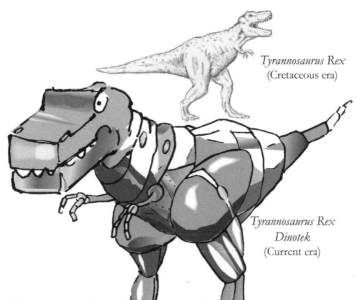

Tyrannosaurus Rex
(Cretaceous era)

Tyrannosaurus Rex Dinotek
(Current era)

The Secret Dinosaur
By N.S.Blackman

Centrosaurus
(Cretaceous era)

Centrosaurus Dinotek
(Current era)

D0800050

Also available in the **Dinoteks** series

The Secret Dinosaur Book 2
The Secret Dinosaur Book 3
The Secret Dinosaur Book 4
The Lost Dinosaur (for younger readers)

Visit www.dinoteks.com for the latest titles, puzzles and activities featuring the Dinoteks!

The Dinoteks

Next time you go to a museum look out for the dusty old dinosaur that nobody else is interested in.

There's usually one.

See it over there in the corner? It looks quite forgotten standing all by itself.

Well maybe it's just waiting for the right person to talk to it...

Giants Awake... introduces the Dinoteks – dinosaurs as you've always dreamed they could be.

www.dinoteks.com

This book is dedicated to
Alice and Thomas
– remembering all the
dinosaur adventures we had together

The very beginning

······················

One Rainy Night

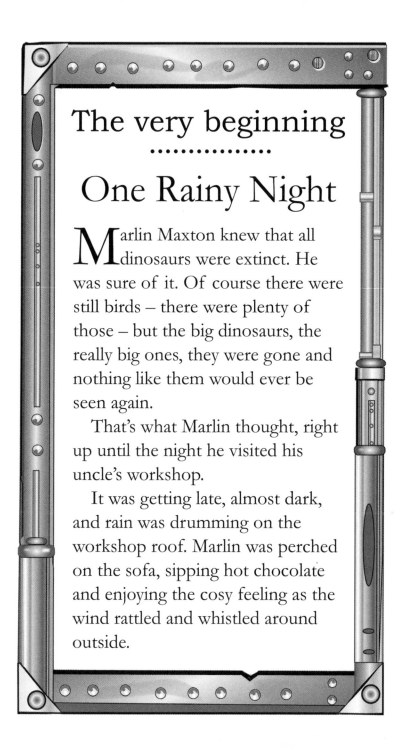

Marlin Maxton knew that all dinosaurs were extinct. He was sure of it. Of course there were still birds – there were plenty of those – but the big dinosaurs, the really big ones, they were gone and nothing like them would ever be seen again.

That's what Marlin thought, right up until the night he visited his uncle's workshop.

It was getting late, almost dark, and rain was drumming on the workshop roof. Marlin was perched on the sofa, sipping hot chocolate and enjoying the cosy feeling as the wind rattled and whistled around outside.

Uncle Gus was always making things – fixing things together and coming up with strange inventions. Some people thought he was foolish – and it's true he was a bit scruffy and more than a bit forgetful – but Marlin knew he was really very clever.

On this particular night Uncle Gus had the parts from a very old engine laid out on the floor, waiting to be repaired. He was sitting completely still, thinking about something (something complicated, probably) when suddenly he looked up.

"School trip to the museum tomorrow, Marlin?" he said. "I wonder if you'll see old Protos?"

He took a sip of his drink and his eyes twinkled at Marlin through the rising steam.

"Protos? Who's that?"

"Who's that?" he laughed. "Did I never tell you?"

Marlin shook his head.

"No."

"That's odd…" frowned Uncle Gus – and he leaned forward. "Never mind, I'll tell you now. Years ago, when I was young,

I thought Protos was the best thing in the museum. He's a metal dinosaur."

A gust of wind rattled the workshop windows and Marlin snuggled into his fleece. He listened as his uncle described the creature.

"Life-size he was – very big – a Centrosaurus. Four legs, thick as

9

tree trunks and a long curving horn right on the front of his nose."

He stretched out his arms, as wide as they would go, to show how long the horn was.

"I remember he used to stand all by himself in his own special room at the back of the dinosaur gallery."

Marlin was eager to hear more but Uncle Gus was now standing up and working on the engine again.

"But what's so special about him?!"

"Eh? Who?"

"Protos!"

Uncle Gus put down his spanner and smiled.

"Well, maybe you'll find out tomorrow. If you see him. But I don't suppose you will. It was all so long ago he's probably not even there now…"

Chapter One

·············

A Boy Goes Hunting

"**Q**uiet everybody! Listen!"
The school group lined up outside the museum and everyone was so excited that Mrs Baxter had to shout to be heard.

The building looked fantastic, six storeys high and covered with carvings of plants and animals.

Right next to Marlin a gigantic stone python was snaking its way up a stone column. It had been coiling its way up there for more than a hundred years, hunting a stone mouse that it would never quite manage to catch…

It was a sunny day and the light sparkled on the museum's arched windows and glass doors.

But unfortunately it also shone on the bald and frowning head of a man in a suit. He was waiting for them at the entrance.

Mr Oliver Grubbler scowled. He did

not like working at the museum. He didn't like the building, or the wonderful things inside it, or the people who came to look at them.

There was just one thing about his job that he did enjoy and that was handing out worksheets. He gave worksheets to every school group that visited.

The whole class groaned when they saw his bulging pile of papers and that made

Grubbler a little bit happier.

As the children filed through the door, one by one, he handed the sheets out.

"No running, no shouting, no touching anything," he growled. Then he added: "You can look at things, but not for too long."

Marlin's heart sank. With all this work there would be no time to hunt for dinosaurs.

******

Marlin rushed to fill in his sheet. There were pages of questions about animals and plants and they seemed to go on forever. But Marlin worked fast and finished in record time. He stuffed his pencil in his bag and looked up. His friends were still writing.

13

"Maybe I could explore for a few minutes..." Marlin thought to himself. "I won't be long..."

That's what he thought.

******

The dinosaur gallery was amazing. Marlin leaned back and stared up at the huge fossil skeletons towering above him. There was a Diplodocus and a Brachiosaurus (even taller) and straight ahead loomed a Stegosaurus, its back lined with jagged-

Cerotopsi

Spino

plates. The bones hung on almost-invisible wires and seemed to float in the air.

Even better were the life-size models. A group of raptors was picking over the carcass of a dead herbivore – and creeping up behind, a fully grown Allosaurus was about to spring on them in a classic ambush attack.

But Marlin searched everywhere and there was no sign of Uncle Gus's special Centrosaurus.

Disappointed, he turned to leave. And

as he did, he noticed the doorway. There was another room, right at the back of the gallery, almost hidden behind a display of fossils. He moved closer. Maybe this was the place…

Somewhere far off a clock struck twelve. Marlin was starting to feel hungry, it would soon be time to go back to his class, but he *had* to find out what was through that doorway.

He crept forwards and peered into the shadows.

Chapter Two

· · · · · · · · · · · · · · · ·

The Forgotten Giant

S ome people looking into that room would just have walked away again. They would have decided there was nothing special about Protos because he wasn't very realistic, not compared with the big models in the main hall. Instead of having life-like, plastic skin he was made completely out of metal: sheets of armour-plate hammered together, bronze and silver, shining softly in the dim light.

Some people would have walked away – but not Marlin.

Marlin could see it straight away. He could see that Protos really was amazing. The soft metal glow of his armour made him seem *more* alive, not less.

Marlin crept forward into the room. He wanted to look closer.

He *had* to look closer!

The creature was built so beautifully. Some of his pieces were riveted together, while others were carefully welded, or held with bolts. Marlin spotted a sign on the wall but when he went over to look he found that it was covered in dust.

Doesn't anyone clean in this room?

It was as if the place had been forgotten. He reached out and wiped away the grime with his sleeve.

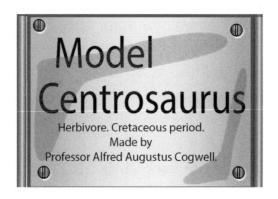

Model
Centrosaurus
Herbivore. Cretaceous period.
Made by
Professor Alfred Augustus Cogwell.

"Model Centrosaurus…" Marlin repeated.

But he knew the sign wasn't quite right.

Protos definitely wasn't just a model, he was a machine. Marlin was certain of it. There were wheels and gears and wires around the creature's back legs and some other parts that had come loose over the years.

He leaned forward to look at the broken bits. He didn't think about what he was doing, and he didn't remember what Mr Grubbler had said about not touching things. He was so used to doing repairs in Uncle Gus's garage that he just started working. He twisted two wires together (making connections) and popped a pin back into place (joining things up). He flicked a switch, and nodded to himself.

"That should do it…"

"I think so," a voice replied. "And if you wouldn't mind screwing the cover back on it helps keep out the dust."

Marlin jumped backwards. He'd been caught!

He stood, his heart racing, and prepared to face the angry museum manager. But instead he found himself looking into the shining glass eye of the dinosaur.

The creature had come to life.

******

The air all around Protos fizzed and crackled with energy – golden sparks flew, as if somebody had set off a firework.

The creature shook himself.

"Ahh! That's better!" Then he blinked.

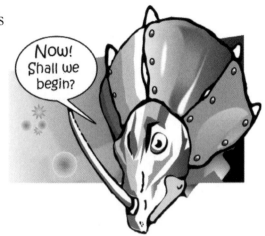

"Is it just you?" he asked. "No-one else?"

He looked around the room. His deep voice sounded disappointed.

"Strange. They told me to expect a few more. Well never mind, the main thing is that you're here. Now! Shall we begin?"

"B…begin?" stuttered Marlin.

"Of course, time is precious, you should never sit around or you might as well be a fossil!"

The machine creature cleared his throat.

"Ahem! Ladies and gentlemen, girls and boys welcome to the Dinoteks Exhibition, the Greatest Show on Earth! My name is Protos and I will be your guide…"

The creature took a heavy, lumbering step forward – CLUNK! – and Marlin

jumped back out of the way.

"Thank you. Now, if you'll kindly follow me..."

Protos moved surprisingly quickly for his size. One of his back legs seemed to drag a bit – and his foot scraped the ground – but he heaved himself forwards happily enough and didn't seem to notice.

"…imagine travelling back through time to the world of the dinosaurs. Close your eyes and think of it. A hundred million years ago – it sounds like a long age but in the life of the Earth that's just the blink of an eye – and in those days our planet was a very different place: a place of wonder, a place of beauty, a place of danger…"

Suddenly Protos stopped, and looked straight at Marlin.

"Speaking of danger," he said, lowering his voice. "Please don't be frightened. The creatures you are about to see are all perfectly safe. I especially want you to remember this when you see Flame, our T-Rex. He may look fierce but he's only acting. Also, don't stand too close to Steg when he turns round, his tail is sharp and no matter how often I remind him he forgets."

He continued out through the door – then stopped again.

"Ah! One other thing. We have a Pterosaur. He's very sweet but if he offers to take you flying, just say no – he can't actually fly you see, he just thinks he can. Got that? Good – this way!"

And Protos was off again.

"Where was I? Ah yes...a place of wonder, a place of beauty, a place of danger. Thanks to the miracle of modern technology, you will see this ancient world brought back to life again. The Dinoteks combine the very latest in intelligent software and sophisticated mechanics..."

CLUNK!

Suddenly a large piece of metal dropped off of Protos's tail and rolled across the floor. He continued walking and didn't seem to notice, so Marlin picked it up for him and quickly pushed it back into place.

"...in fact, Ladies and Gentlemen, the Dinoteks are living, thinking creatures, just like you..."

Protos paused and looked over his shoulder.

"Actually, I won't bother with all that 'Ladies and Gentlemen' stuff if you don't mind. It seems a bit silly as there's only one of you. What *is* your name?"

"Marlin."

"Marlin! That's better. Now, follow me Marlin and try to keep up…"

Protos lumbered right across the dinosaur gallery and to Marlin's surprise didn't stop there. He went out through a door and into a long, narrow passage.

"Er, shouldn't we be back in the dinosaur gallery?" Marlin asked.

"In that old place? No, no – the Dinoteks Show is much better than that! Come along now, this way…"

The corridor they were now in looked much older than the rest of the museum and Marlin noticed that the floor was covered in dust, just like the sign on the wall in Protos' room. The passage was poorly lit, and in several places cobwebs dangled from the ceiling.

"…now prepare to be amazed. As we step through these doors, you will think you have journeyed back through time!"

There were double doors right in front of them, twice as big as ordinary doors. Protos stopped and looked at Marlin. His eyes were sparkling with excitement.

"Ready Marlin?"

"Er, ready – I think..."

"Then follow me!"

He lowered his great armoured head and shoved against the doors. The hinges strained for a moment then gave a loud, rusty crack and swung open.

"Welcome to the greatest show on earth!" Protos announced.

And in they both went.

Chapter Three

· · · · · · · · · · · · · · ·

The Lost Room

The room was a mess. It was dark. Piles of junk were heaped up everywhere and a thick layer of dust covered the floor. Protos looked around confused.

"Flame! Steg! Are you ready?"

But there was no reply.

"Dacky? Come on everybody! Our first visitor is here! We need to start the show…"

His voice trailed off. It echoed into silence. The old creature stood there looking around him and in that moment Marlin felt very sorry for him.

"I don't understand…"

Marlin came to stand next to him.

"I think something went wrong," he said gently. "How long did you say you've been waiting for your show to begin?"

"How long? Let me see…it was Friday afternoon…the Professor said everything was nearly finished and…" Protos frowned, confused. "I waited…then I took a quick nap and then…then you woke me up."

The creature looked at him.

"It can't have been *very* long… can it?"

Marlin went back to the door and fumbled around for a light switch. He flicked it on – to reveal an amazing collection of metal dinosaurs, all around the room. But they were all covered in dust, from head to toe. It had settled on them layer by layer, year by year, burying them like fossils.

"I…I remember now…" Protos said quietly. "I waited, but the Professor didn't come … I kept waiting…I kept looking out for him…but then I fell asleep…"

He looked at Marlin.

"That's it, isn't it? I've been asleep for years."

And a great, oily tear rolled down his metal face.

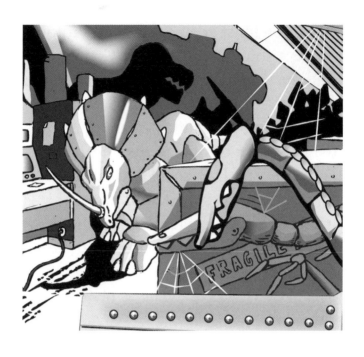

******

Marlin sat with the old Centrosaurus for a long time in the lost room. The creature shuffled around trying to tidy things up, and Marlin helped him. But it was no use, there was too much mess.

Then, far off, he heard a bell and suddenly he remembered his class – he had to get back. He would be in trouble!

"Yes, you must go at once," said Protos. "I've kept you talking too long. Come on..."

And he heaved himself round and cleared his throat.

"Ladies and Gentlemen – I mean Marlin – thank you for coming to the Greatest Show on Earth. I am sorry that due to technical difficulties the Dinoteks were not able to continue with today's show. I do hope this didn't spoil your visit to the museum too much…"

His back leg was dragging as he headed for the door.

"Wait!" cried Marlin, running after him. "My visit to the museum wasn't spoiled and I don't care that the show couldn't happen!"

Protos looked at him and smiled.

"Thank you Marlin. I'm glad it was you who came to our first show. It was nice meeting you and – "

Then suddenly there was a loud BANG and a wisp of smoke curled around Protos's leg. He looked down.

"Oh dear," he whispered. "I think that was my battery…can't stay awake…"

He looked up and smiled.

"Thank you for coming Ladies and Gentlemen…I mean Marlin…"

And that was the last word he said. His head nodded, his eyes closed.

"Wait!" exclaimed Marlin. "Don't sleep! Tell me how to help you!"

But Protos didn't reply. He stood there like all his friends, no longer alive but just a statue.

******

Marlin sprinted down the old corridor and back through the dinosaur gallery to find his class. His mind was racing. He had to find a way to help Protos. He couldn't just leave him standing there, forever forgotten…

He was so busy trying to think of what to do that he didn't notice Oliver Grubbler step out in front of him and he went smack into the big man's stomach.

"Whoa! Where do you think you're going boy?!"

"I…I got lost!" exclaimed Marlin. "I'm looking for my class!"

Grubbler rubbed his stomach and glared at him suspiciously.

"It's that way," he grunted, jabbing his finger towards the exit. "And no running!"

Relieved, Marlin walked away as quickly as he dared. Grubbler called after him.

"I've got my eye on you!"

Chapter Four

The Thing That All Machines Hate

Marlin tried to tell his teacher what had happened, but she was too busy to listen.

"Line up with the others now, or we'll be late!" she said firmly.

When he got home his mum and dad were too busy to listen too. They were loading boxes into their car, getting ready for another business trip. His mum smiled as she hurried past.

Marlin realised there was only one person who would listen: Uncle Gus. The quickest way to his workshop was down the garden, over the fence and along an alleyway.

Marlin sprinted all the way.

The workshop was a little brick building, covered in ivy, with a patched-up roof of rusty metal. It nestled in the shadow of an oak tree and a rope had been looped over one of the branches, with a tyre for Marlin to swing on.

A friendly orange light was peeping out through the workshop's open door.

A few minutes later Uncle Gus listened in silence as Marlin told his story. He looked thoughtful and nodded from time to time. His bushy eyebrows were set in a deep frown.

Marlin had never seen him look quite so serious.

"You're sure? The old dinosaur really came to life lad?"

Marlin nodded.

"And he spoke to you?"

"Yes!"

Then Uncle Gus chuckled.

"Well that's very odd. Very odd indeed. I've been talking to my car for years but she never answers me!"

He hurried across the workshop to a shelf piled with junk.

"Where is it, where is it now? …Aha!"

He turned round smiling and handed Marlin an old cloth bag.

"The question is," he said "what are you going to do about these Dinoteks now?"

"I really want to help them," Marlin answered. "But I don't know how!"

"Then what you need is a *plan*."

He rubbed his hands together happily and stood thinking. Uncle Gus liked making plans, and they were usually very good ones. Marlin waited hopefully.

Uncle Gus spoke at last.

"I can't tell you exactly what to do," he said. "But I can tell you where to start. Do you remember last year when we took that old steam engine apart? We cleaned all the pieces, made some repairs, then put everything back together?"

Marlin nodded.

"Do you remember – what is the one thing that all machines hate?" asked Uncle Gus.

Marlin thought about it.

"Dirt?"

"That's right lad – brilliant boy! Dirt and dust! It gets right into them, see? And stops them working."

Now Uncle Gus nodded at the cloth bag that he'd given Marlin. Marlin looked inside: there was a pile of rags, three jars of metal cleaner and a big can of machine oil.

******

Cleaning the Dinoteks was a big job and Marlin went back to the museum every evening for two weeks.

He went straight after school and crept through the galleries to the hidden passage. He made sure nobody was looking – especially the horrible Mr Grubbler – then pushed hard on the big double doors. They creaked at first and did not want to move but then a gap opened for him to squeeze through.

Each day he had with him his cleaning bag and his lunchbox so he wouldn't get hungry.

Each day he went home again at six o'clock.

"Working late today?" his mum would say.

Marlin always answered yes (which was true) and she never actually asked what he was working on.

"Keep it up," his dad would say, patting him on the back.

******

Now something strange happened. Marlin discovered that cleaning could be fun.

Of course he never liked tidying up at home, but here in the secret room he was happy to wipe off grime, scrape out dirt, wash, brush and polish. It was exciting

He cleaned the Dinoteks one by one and he dripped machine oil into their joints. He started with the two little ones (the Troodons), then the Pterosaur and then he went on to the giants.

When he got to the Stegosaurus he needed a ladder to reach its armoured back-plates.

What do all machines hate? Dirt and dust!
Monday
Tuesday
Wednesday
Thursday
Friday
Phew...don't you T-Rexs ever wash?!

Finally he worked on Protos and then the T-Rex, which towered over all of them.

Marlin tried to remember what Protos had called him…*Flame, wasn't it? Flame, yes that was it.*

"Time to wake up Flame…" Marlin said softly as he cleaned.

******

Day by day the dinosaurs looked less like old fossils. Their metal skins began to glow.

They were coming back to life.

Chapter Five

· · · · · · · · · · · · · · · · ·

Something Goes Click!

Now the secret room wasn't gloomy any more. Now it really was magical, just as Protos had promised. Everything was glowing, even the metal trees with their hanging branches danced and shimmered with life.

Just one thing spoiled it.

The Dinoteks stayed frozen.

Marlin had worked hard. He had cleaned the creatures from top to bottom. He had done everything Uncle Gus had told him, but it seemed to make no difference.

All the time Marlin kept hoping to hear a friendly voice suddenly boom out and see those sparkling lights like little fireworks again.

But it didn't happen.

"There must be something else," he said to himself. "Something I need to do. Something I haven't thought of…"

And he was saying these exact words – "something I haven't thought of" – when it happened.

There was a click.

Yes – he was wiping his polishing cloth over the Protos's front leg and *something clicked*.

A metal plate moved under his hand and then popped open on a hinge! Marlin leaned forward to look. There was a space full of wires. And in the middle of that space was a grey cylinder. It had silver tips at each end.

Marlin reached in. The cylinder was smooth and cold.

"It looks like…like a huge battery…"

He gave the cylinder a tug and it came loose in his hand. It was very heavy.

A battery…

What if all the Dinoteks have them?

He ran over to the Stegosaurus and pressed his leg in the same way – a hatch popped open. There was another space exactly the same, a tangle of wires and a long grey cylinder.

And when he searched each one of the other creatures he found the same thing.

This has to be the answer!

Quickly, he pulled out all the cylinders and tucked them into his bag. Then he heaved it over his shoulder. It was really heavy but he knew what he had to do.

He would carry the cylinders to Uncle Gus.

******

"You're right!" beamed his uncle. "I haven't seen batteries like this for years – in fact I can't remember when I last did."

He was holding one up to the light, peering at it.

"What a lucky find – magnificent! One of these would give your creatures all the power they need – if it was fully charged…"

He shoved the battery back into Marlin's hand and began searching for something at the back of the workshop. A moment later he was dragging a wooden crate out from under a workbench.

Marlin rushed to help.

"That's right lad, let's get it into the light…"

At last, when the crate was out in the open, Marlin could see that it was very old and heaped full of junk, tools and strange bits of machinery.

Uncle Gus began rummaging through it, pulling things out.

"Let me see now …I'm sure I put it in here…AHA!"

He stood up triumphantly, clutching a golden box. It had two handles, one on each side, two clips hanging from it on wires and a little dial on the front like a clock-face.

"It's a universal power-charger," he

explained. "It's a very clever tool. I invented it myself — I can't quite remember why, but I'm sure it must have been for something important…"

He picked up the cylinder battery again and attached the clips to it, one to each silver tip.

At first nothing happened. Uncle Gus peered intently at the clock face.

"Come on now…don't let me down…"

Then suddenly the needle twitched and began to move around the dial.

"Aha! That's more like it!"

Uncle Gus beamed and gave the golden machine a gentle pat.

"It's powering up Marlin. What did I tell you? This little beauty will bring anything back to life."

Marlin grinned. "How long will it take?"

"Oh, not long lad, not long. Come back in the morning. By then I'll have all your batteries working perfectly."

****

That night Marlin had a fantastic dream. In it, he arrived at the museum to find Protos standing at the door waiting for him, his polished skin glowing brightly.

"Welcome to the Great Dinotek Show!" exclaimed the dream creature. "Everybody's waiting for you inside. Except for Dacky. Look up there! I admit I'm a bit surprised, but guess what? He can fly after all!"

Marlin looked up and saw the Pterosaur swooping round far, far above the museum. As the creature crossed the sky the sun glinted on his golden head-crest.

He was clutching a banner in his claws.

'Dinoteks Show Now Open!' said the writing on the banner. 'All Welcome!"

"Wait here!" exclaimed Marlin. "I'm going to get all my friends!"

And in his dream, with his heart racing, he rushed off to school to tell the whole class.

And that's when he woke up.

That happy dream lingered in his mind and he lay in bed smiling. Then he remembered why it was he felt so excited.

Today, the batteries would be ready.
Today it would really happen.

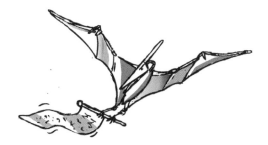

Chapter Six

••••••••••••••••••

Telling Lies
and
Telling the Truth

The sun was shining brightly and it was time to wake the Dinoteks. Marlin was standing in the doorway of the secret room and his heart was racing.

Now, the most sensible thing for him to do next would be to wake Protos first, *not* the big T-Rex.

And that's what he nearly did. He nearly went straight over to the Centrosaurus, clicked the battery into place and waited for him to come to life.

But as he stood there staring at the

Dinoteks, it was the T-Rex that he was really looking at. In fact he couldn't take his eyes off it.

Maybe it was because the towering creature had taken so long to clean. Or maybe he thought it would be nice for Protos to wake up and find one of his friends already awake and waiting for him.

Maybe.

Or perhaps it was something else. There was something about the golden-headed predator that drew Marlin forwards and made him want to plug the battery in. He wanted to do it even though his hands were trembling just a bit.

He stepped up to the huge clawed foot.

"OK," he whispered. "I'll just see what happens if…"

And that's as far as he got. Because a meaty hand clapped down on his shoulder.

"Caught you at last!" growled Mr Grubbler.

Marlin jumped up – but the museum manager held him tight.

******

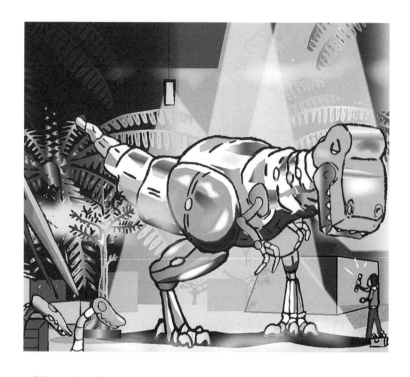

Marlin sat miserably in Oliver Grubbler's office. He was alone and the door was locked.

After ordering him to sit down Grubbler had stomped off without a word. His footsteps had faded and then the room plunged into silence.

Now Marlin sat alone and it was so quiet he felt his heart beating. He wished he had a phone to call Uncle Gus.

He waited and it felt as if he was waiting

51

forever, until at last the heavy footsteps returned. For an instant Marlin wondered whether he should hide under the desk but it was too late. A key stabbed and rattled in the lock and the door swung open.

"I've got him trapped in here, Inspector…"

Grubbler stepped in and pointed at him.

"Here he is. This is the thief!"

A woman leaned in behind him and peered at Marlin. She had grey hair and dark, stern eyes.

"Hmm. He doesn't look like a thief Mr Grubbler. He looks like a child."

Grubbler snorted.

"Don't be fooled! When you run a busy museum you soon learn that children and criminals are often the same thing."

The woman didn't reply to that. She came and sat on a chair next to Marlin.

"My name is Inspector Bailey," she said. "I'm a police detective."

Her eyes were very serious but her voice was kind and Marlin began to feel a little less afraid.

"Mr Grubbler says you've been creeping into the museum and stealing things. Have you?"

Marlin hesitated, unsure what to say. He knew his story would sound like it was made up. Across the room he could see Mr Grubbler staring at him.

Marlin decided to tell the truth.

"I haven't stolen anything. I've been repairing the dinosaurs. I want to bring them back to life."

Inspector Bailey's eyebrows lifted.

"Ha!" laughed Grubbler. "See? He's a liar as well as a thief!"

But the detective kept looking at Marlin.

"How could you bring dinosaurs back to life?" she asked.

Marlin took a deep breath.

"Because I'm not talking about fossils – I'm talking about machines, living machines."

******

Marlin took the detective and the museum manager back to the secret room. Mr Grubbler stood by the door with his arms obstinately folded while Inspector Bailey walked among the Dinoteks.

"And you say you cleaned all these machines up? All by yourself?"

"Yes."

She was staring up at the T-Rex in wonder.

"When I found them they were covered in dust. I don't think anyone even knew they were here."

He pointed to the cloth bag that was still on the floor where he'd left it.

"I was about to put their batteries in and wake them up."

"That's a lie!" exclaimed Grubbler. "And anyway, this room has always been perfectly clean. There's never any mess in my museum!"

Inspector Bailey thought about this. She had noticed there was a lot of grime on the floor in the corridor leading to this room. And she had also spotted some very strange footprints there. They were very large footprints. Of course the boy's story about waking up dinosaurs was silly, but...

She looked thoughtfully at Marlin and then leaned down to pick up one of the grey cylinders from the bag.

"Well it certainly looks like a battery," she

said. "I suppose there's only one way to find out…"

She handed the cylinder to Marlin.

"Would you like to plug it in?"

Mr Grubbler gasped and backed away towards the door.

"Really Inspector!" he spluttered. "I'm not sure that's a good idea…"

But quickly, before the detective could change her mind, Marlin hurried over to the T-Rex. He pushed the battery into its leg and – CLICK! – it snapped into place.

Marlin flipped the cover shut and stepped immediately back, like somebody lighting the fuse on a dangerous firework.

Then all three of them held their breath.

Chapter Seven

·············

Dinosaur Clues

Inspector Bailey's car rolled smoothly up the hill towards Marlin's house. She was giving him a ride home. He sat slumped in the passenger seat and felt miserable.

The T-Rex hadn't moved.

"Don't worry Marlin, I know you're not a thief," Inspector Bailey said. "But it's probably best if you keep away from the museum for a while. No point upsetting Mr Grubbler."

"OK," Marlin nodded.

The detective glanced at him and smiled.

"When I was your age I loved

dinosaurs too. I used to wish they'd come to life."

Marlin wanted to tell her it wasn't just a wish – it was real – but instead he just nodded.

He liked her. He didn't want her to think he was a liar.

******

For once Uncle Gus wasn't in his workshop – the lights were all off and the door was locked.

Marlin's parents weren't home yet so he made himself a sandwich and sat staring gloomily out of the window.

Why hadn't it worked? Why had the T-Rex not come to life? As soon as Uncle Gus came home Marlin would ask him.

Across the road the lights came on in his friend Daniel's house. Marlin decided to go and see him instead.

Daniel was setting up a train track for his little brother Max, so Marlin joined in. When it was ready they showed Max how to use the trains to push marbles around.

It was a good game and Marlin forgot his gloomy mood. But then one of the trains began to slow down.

"Quick," said Daniel. "Let's change the battery."

And Marlin's heart sank because that reminded him again about the Dinoteks.

He sighed. It was getting dark outside anyway, and time for him to go. He said goodbye and headed back across the road.

But as he walked something strange happened. He had a very odd feeling that he was being watched. He glanced around. The road was empty.

"I'm just tired," he told himself.

And that's when he tripped over the broken paving stone.

"Ouch!

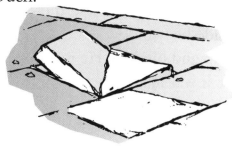

He picked himself up and looked at it. The stone was cracked clean in half and one edge was sticking up. It was as if something unusually heavy had pressed down on it.

Funny...I'm sure it wasn't like that before.

He pushed the edge down with his foot so nobody else would trip. Then he hurried on into his house.

He didn't notice that the paving stone wasn't the only thing mysteriously damaged. Just down the road a lamppost was glowing with a friendly orange light. But it was strangely bent – about half way up – as if something very large had bumped into it.

******

Marlin woke up suddenly. It was the middle of the night and there was a noise outside his window.

He sat up and blinked. He was dreaming. No! There it was again!

TAP...TAP TAP...TAP...

He slipped out of bed and crept over to the curtains. The floor was cold under his feet and the air was chilly but he hardly noticed.

He reached out with one finger and nudged a crack in the curtains.

WOOOOOSH!

Something very fast flashed past – silver in the moonlight – and was gone.

Marlin jumped back, his heart racing.

"What was that?!"

He edged forwards again. He pulled the curtains open wider this time and peered out.

At first he saw nothing but then he noticed the strange marks on the lawn. All over, the grass was churned up and muddy as if something heavy had been racing around on it.

Then he saw it.

A creature standing at the end of the garden.

Just under the apple tree, next to the garden gate, was a little silver dinosaur with a long whip tail and a slender neck.
It cocked its head to one side, blinked and looked right at him.

There was no mistaking it. It was one of the Troodons from the museum.

Chapter Eight

· · · · · · · · · · · · · · ·

Into the Night

No time to get dressed! Marlin shoved on his sweater and ran to the back door. He stuck his bare feet into his trainers.

Through the window he could still see it – the creature was still under the apple tree.

It had lowered its head and was sniffing around in the grass, poking its nose at something – a fallen apple?

Marlin opened the door – CLICK! – and its head jerked up. The Troodon stared at him with its bright, glass eyes.

Marlin took a step forward, very slowly so as not to frighten it. He held his hands gently out in front of him.

"Hello…hello there…"

The creature stood totally still.

"My name is Marlin…don't be frightened…"

He was half way across the lawn and the Troodon had still not moved.

"…what's your name?…"

Marlin edged forward again.

But before he could take another step something huge loomed over him and grabbed him from behind.

He went up.

His stomach lurched, the ground fell away and suddenly he was looking down on the world from a great height. The little creature, now far below, blinked up at him.

It turned with a flick of its tail and ran off.

Then Marlin felt himself being thrown upwards. He twisted in the air for a second before two steel jaws snapped shut around him.

******

It was dark and a cold wind rushed over him. But Marlin guessed exactly where he was.

Rows of teeth surrounded him like prison bars. He was inside the mouth of the Dinotek T-Rex.

The creature was running very fast, away from his house. Through the gaps between the teeth Marlin could see the world outside racing by, trees, buildings, lights, all flying past incredibly quickly.

But he couldn't look properly because with each thunderous step he was bounced around, this way and that.

He reached out and grabbed one of the teeth.

"Stop!" he shouted. "Put me down!"

But the creature ignored him and raced on.

Chapter Nine

· · · · · · · · · · · · · ·

Voices in the Dark

The T-Rex was slowing down. The footsteps now became a stomping walk and the wind stopped blowing.

Then Marlin heard voices. Strange voices – clucking, cawing and not-quite-human.

"It's Flame! And Siggy! They're back – open the doors!" called one.

"Inside everyone, quick, get out of sight!" came another.

The great jaws holding Marlin lowered. The teeth parted, and he was tipped sprawling onto the ground.

It was cold and dark – too dark to see a thing – and now the voices were chattering all around him.

It was the Dinoteks, Marlin was sure of it. They were all here except for Protos. His deep and gentle voice wasn't one of them.

"Is this really him? Is this the thief?" (*A sharp voice – was that the Stegosaurus?*)

"Of course it is!" (*A rumbling voice – definitely the T-Rex*). "The trail was easy to follow. I could smell him even out there."

"And I tricked him!" (*A voice so small it was almost a squeak – obviously a Troodon*). "I tricked him into coming out!"

"That's true, Siggy had a good idea there," replied the deep voice. "I wanted to bite the roof off the house but he just tapped on the window and the thief came out!"

"The thief is very small," the sharp voice said. "I thought he would be bigger."

"All humans are small," the big voice replied.

"But what's it like? Out there? On the outside?" This was a new voice. It cawed, like a crow. (*Wings? The Pterosaur?*)

"The outside is big," rumbled the reply. "You think this place where we live is

68

big but it's not. Outside there are more buildings just like it. More than you can count, and they go on forever."

"With lots of corridors in between!" added the squeaky voice.

"Roads," corrected the big one. "They're called roads. And that's where the danger is. Humans go on the roads in their cars, very fast. We were nearly spotted a few times."

"And we nearly got lost. We had to run," added the squeaky one. "But nobody saw us!"

"Very good, you did well," said the sharp voice, coming closer to Marlin. "But now – the main thing is we've caught him."

Something prodded Marlin's leg. He scrambled to his feet. He felt bruised but he had no broken bones.

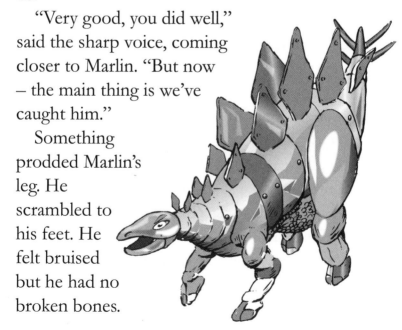

"Well? What have you done with it?"

A light came on and Marlin squinted in the sudden brightness, trying to see.

A giant shadow leaned over him, armour plates towering up like jagged rocks. It was the creature with the sharp voice – it was the Stegosaurus. The T-Rex stood behind him, leaning in close.

"I don't know what you mean…" protested Marlin.

"Don't you? Really?" snapped the Stegosaurus. "Follow me!"

He turned and flicked his spiked-tail. Then he marched across the room. The others crowded after him, herding Marlin between them.

There, standing in the shadows, was Protos.

Marlin ran over to him. But the old Centrosaurus was frozen still, his head bowed and his eyes closed.

"We want to know where Protos's battery is – where is the battery that *you* stole?"

Chapter Ten

· · · · · · · · · · · · · ·

The Thief!

Marlin stood there and the dinosaurs crowded around, their metal plates rattling as they jostled to see him.

"Well?" demanded the Stegosaurus. "What have you got to say?"

Marlin looked up at them all – and he felt very small standing there. He felt himself trembling. But suddenly he realised that he wasn't frightened. No, he wasn't afraid – he was actually feeling angry. After all his hard work, this just wasn't fair!

"Now listen to me and stop talking!" he exclaimed. "I'm not a thief. I'm here to help you!"

The Stegosaurus took a step back, frowning.

The other Dinoteks backed away too, all except the T-Rex. He squinted suspiciously at Marlin.

"Now then! Don't try any tricks," he growled. "Just answer the question."

"I'm not tricking you," said Marlin. "It is true I took all your batteries, but only to power them up. Then I brought them all back. They were in that bag."

He pointed across the room. The cloth bag was still on the floor exactly where he'd left it.

"Hmm... I did find all your batteries in that bag," growled the T-Rex.

"He could be telling the truth I suppose…"

"So if he's telling the truth, where is Protos's battery now?" demanded the Steg.

"Where I left it, of course," answered Marlin.

He went over to the bag and snatched it up. But it was empty.

"I don't understand…"

He looked at the metal creatures.

"Somebody else must have taken it!"

The Stegosaurus snorted. But the T-Rex stepped forward. He pushed his great nose down and sniffed at the bag.

"Maybe you're right," he said. "I *can* smell something else. Another human…"

Marlin suddenly had an idea. And it seemed such a definite idea that he was sure he was right about it.

There was only one person who could have come in here: Oliver Grubbler!

The T-Rex was sniffing, trying to catch the scent, to follow it.

"The trail leads this way…"

He paced across the room to stand by the window.

"Somewhere over there," he said grimly. "It's a long way off…"

They crowded round him and looked out into the dark. Far away, over the rooftops of the city, was a single building standing higher than all the others.

It was a great glass tower.

******

"**I** can see the battery!" exclaimed Dacky suddenly, making everyone jump.

"What?!" snapped Steg.

"At the top of that tower! There's a room. I can see humans, lots of them, all sitting around a table – and they have the battery, right there!"

"Nobody can see that far," snorted Steg.

"I can," cawed Dacky. "Superior vision is a well-known power of the Pterosaurs."

He unfurled his wings, and shook them. They stretched wide, filling half the room, like the sails of a great ship.

"I also have speed," he said. "So watch! Now I will fly to the glass tower and get the battery!"

He strode forwards, beat his wings – once, twice – and tripped over. His silver body sprawled awkwardly on the floor.

******

The T-Rex leaned down to help him.

"You can't really fly, Dacky, remember?" he said gently. "Don't worry,

I'll go outside again."

"I…I wanted to help…" cawed the winged reptile, struggling to his feet

"You did help," said Flame. "Thanks to your eyes I now know exactly where to go. Comp and Siggy will help me." The two Troodons gave an excited squeak. The T-Rex strode over to the door and they scampered close behind him.

"But be careful," Steg snapped after them. "This could be very dangerous. Remember you're not going out into quiet roads. This time you're going right into the middle of the city and if the humans see you, they'll try to hunt you."

"We'll be careful," said Flame, grimly.

One of little Troodons nodded – was that one Siggy? – but the other looked nervous.

All of Dinoteks had forgotten about Marlin, who was still standing holding the empty bag.

He stepped forward.

"Wait!" he called. "I can help!"

******

Flame, the golden-headed T-Rex, looked down at Marlin.

"You want to help us?! But you're so small," he growled. "And you're not even dressed properly."

It was true. Marlin was beginning to feel quite cold.

"Hah!" cawed Dacky. "I can fix that."

He flapped across the room and a moment later came back with a big bundle clutched in his beak. He dropped it at Marlin's feet.

"There! It's from my favourite part of the museum, the Flight Gallery."

Marlin unwrapped the bundle. It was a leather pilot's jacket. It was certainly large, made for an adult, but it might just fit. He tried it, and it did, hanging almost to his knees. It was lined with wool and it felt snug and warm. And there was a pair of goggles to pull over his eyes.

"I'll look like an old-fashioned racing driver," he laughed putting them on.

"Good. Because you'll be going fast," answered Flame.

And before Marlin could argue, the T-Rex bent down, picked him up, and threw him into the air.

It must have been a very skilful throw because Marlin somersaulted and landed perfectly on the great creature's back. He gasped and held out his arms to keep his balance.

"Look in front of you," Steg called up to him.

Marlin looked down at the T-Rex's back and at first saw nothing. Then he spotted it: a leather strap with a buckle.

"Undo the buckle and lift up the flap," ordered Steg.

Marlin did it. Underneath the flap there was a small space in the T-Rex's back, like the cockpit of an aeroplane. And there, inside it, was a seat!

"In you pop," chuckled Flame. "It'll be much better than carrying you in my mouth. And this time we'll be able to talk to each other!"

Marlin grinned and slipped down into the seat. He did feel like a racing driver now, but this was going to be much better than riding in a car.

He was about to go racing on a T-Rex.

Chapter Eleven

·················

Faster, Faster, FASTER!

The wind rushed past with a roar, catching Marlin's breath.

He pulled the racing goggles on so he could face straight into it without blinking.

"WOAH!"

This was the most thrilling thing he'd ever done!

"Hold on tight!" called Flame.

He began the journey with two great strides – THUD! THUD! – then they left the museum behind and he picked up speed.

He leaned forwards, his head dropped low and he began to accelerate. Then his legs became a blur.

Behind them, the two little

Troodons skittered along, racing to keep up but not quite managing it. And every few seconds Flame looked back. Each time he did, Marlin could feel him slow down for them.

Wow! How fast would this T-Rex go if he *wasn't* waiting for anyone?!

They crossed the city in no time, keeping to quiet roads and ducking into the shadows whenever a car appeared.

They jumped over a fence and then ran across a park, between trees. Now they were running on open grass, across a hillside, with sky all around them.

Suddenly Marlin knew what it must have been like for the prehistoric Tyrannosaurs sprinting across the wide, endless plains of the Jurassic. He closed his eyes and it was as if he really was back in that other time. It was a feeling of such freedom and excitement that he wanted it to go on forever.

But already Flame was slowing down.

"There it is," the T-Rex nodded.

The glass tower was there, right in front of them. Marlin stared up at it, glittering against the sky. Now it looked huge.

It was brightly lit, and all the area around it was lit-up too – there was a car park in front, but it was empty of cars.

"Hmmm…there's nowhere here to hide here," muttered Flame.

"Yes there is, look!" replied Marlin.

On the far side, half in shadow, was a grassy bank. Flame nodded.

"Good, let's get over there and out of sight."

The Troodons followed and they all huddled together and looked up at the tower.

"What now?" squeaked Comp.

Marlin suddenly felt nervous. Now they'd arrived he didn't know what to do – only that this was the most important part of the mission.

"I'll go," he said.

Flame nodded.

"Good. I think it's a job for a human. But be careful. Get in and out as fast as you can."

Marlin climbed out of the seat and slid down the T-Rex's tail. He turned towards the tower. This was it.

******

The way in was through a glass door. On the other side of the glass Marlin could

see there was a desk…and a chair…and
sitting there, a man in a uniform. It was the
building's security guard – and he looked
big.

What now? He'll never let me inside…

But suddenly he had an idea! He called
over his shoulder.

"Siggy? Can you do that trick again, like you did on me? Can you get the guard to come out?"

The Troodon blinked and nodded. And his tail wagged happily.

******

The security guard's name was Buster Crank. His two favourite treats in life were breaking things and eating sausages. He only broke things if he was allowed to break them (which didn't happen very often) but at least he had sausages every day. He liked all sorts, even vegetarian ones.

He was thinking about sausages when something silver flashed past outside. He saw it, just for a second, then it was gone.

He frowned and tried to get back to thinking about sausages. He thought about how nice they smelled when they were sizzling in his pan…how cosy they sounded as they crackled…how good they tasted when he took the first bite…

But then the silver thing went past again. Or was it a different silver thing? It went

84

very fast. And he even thought it had legs…

"Right! I'd better go and look."

He got up and opened the glass door. He stepped outside and peered around. He pointed with his torch. But he couldn't see the silver thing at all now.

"Very strange that is…"

He didn't notice the young boy slipping through the door behind him.

******

Marlin got into the lift. It was new and shiny and the doors closed with a gentle swish. He looked at all the buttons, then pressed the highest number, hoping that would take him to the top floor.

Up he went.

The doors hissed open again and he stepped out into an empty corridor. There were doors on both sides, all closed. But right ahead he could hear voices talking. And there was one door, just open a crack.

He crept closer and suddenly he saw it. The battery was inside that room – Protos's battery!

It was so close he could almost reach it.

But the room was full of people. They were having a big meeting. And it was going to be a long meeting because there was a tea trolley next to the door, loaded with nice things to eat and drink.

He thought about what to do.

He could just rush in and grab the battery.

Or he could creep in quietly, keeping low and hope nobody noticed. They were all so busy talking that he might just get away with it.

Or he might not.

His heart was beating fast and his mouth had gone dry. He really didn't want to go into that room with all those people but he knew he must.

He remembered Protos's words – "I'm glad it was *you* Marlin…"

Thinking of the Centrosaurus made him more determined. And suddenly he had an idea.

******

The tea trolley was next to the door, piled up with cups, saucers, pots of tea and a big plate of chocolate biscuits. Before he could change his mind Marlin grabbed the trolley and wheeled it straight into the room.

"Tea anyone?" he announced cheerfully.

Everyone stopped talking and looked at him, puzzled. For a horrible moment Marlin thought somebody would demand to know who he was. But he carried on with his act and began putting cups and saucers on the table.

It worked.

One by one the eyes turned away from him. The talking began again.

"Yes, yes" sniffed a man at one end of

the table. "I agree with Mr Grubbler. Let's sell them…"

Marlin worked his way around the table – cup, saucer, cup, saucer – and was careful not to look at anyone.

"…do you know how much money we'd get for them?"

Cup, saucer, cup, saucer…

"A very good question," agreed a grey-haired man (*the Mayor?*). "We should certainly try for the best price…"

Marlin had gone right round the table and so far his plan was working well. But the next part would be the hardest. He wheeled the trolley towards Grubbler and the battery.

"I've made a few phone calls," Grubbler was saying. "And nobody wants them as they are. It's not surprising, they don't look very good. I almost gave up. But then I called Mr Snickenbacker…"

"The scrap metal millionaire?"

"Yes, that's right…"

Marlin put a cup in front of Grubbler and felt the cold battery brush the back of his hand…

"Snickenbacker's offering a very good price…"

This was it. Time for Marlin to try his plan. He picked up the plate of biscuits and slid it into the middle of the table.

Immediately, all eyes were on it, and people began leaning forward greedily, reaching out for a biscuit. In that same moment Marlin scooped up the battery and turned for the door.

"Yes," continued Grubbler, now chomping noisily. "He said he'll buy them and break them up for scrap. That's the only thing those old dinosaurs are good for."

Marlin froze. *Dinosaurs? – the Dinoteks! –* that's what these people were talking about and he hadn't realised it!

"No! You can't!" he gasped. "You can't sell them for scrap!"

And then everyone looked at him.

"You!" roared Grubbler, jumping to his feet.

Marlin shoved the tea trolley at him and ran.

Chapter Twelve

·················

The Wrong Way Stairs

"What's happening now? What can you see?" demanded Steg.

Dacky was peering at the tower, telling them what Marlin was doing. Suddenly he gasped, flapping his wings wide with alarm.

"What's wrong? What is it?!"

"It's the boy!" the Pterosaur cawed. "They're chasing him!"

******

Marlin sprinted down the corridor and Grubbler's heavy footsteps thundered behind him. He was getting closer.

"Stop you little thief! Give that back!"

But Marlin held tightly on to the battery.

He threw himself to one side just as Grubbler was about to grab him.

Marlin stopped sharply but Grubbler couldn't! He was bigger and heavier and went crashing on down the corridor.

Marlin doubled back and pushed open a door. Stairs – but they were leading the wrong way, upwards, not down! He had no choice but to go up. Grubbler was coming again and now Marlin could hear more shouts too as others joined the chase. He dashed up the stairs two at a time and threw himself through another door at the top.

Cold night air hit him. He looked about, confused. Then he realised where he was: on the roof! The lights of the city were shining all around him and below him. Up here on top of the tower he was above everything.

Quick! Find another way out...

He sprinted across the flat open roof, looking around, but there were no other doors.

He reached the edge.

Far below in the car park he could see the golden-headed T-Rex pacing up and down and the Troodons beside him. They were tiny but even from this far away Flame still looked big.

Marlin thought about calling out to him. But, for all the T-Rex's size and speed, what would he be able to do from down there?

He looked at the battery and looked down to the ground. Maybe he could throw it down? Maybe Flame could catch it?

But what if it breaks?!

"Hah! Got you!"

Grubbler came crashing through the door onto the roof. He stood there for a moment just grinning, then he rushed forwards.

******

"H e's trapped! Caught!" Dacky had been watching Marlin on the roof and he saw Grubbler attack. Now he lifted his head and cawed at the sky in despair.

He shook his useless wings – and at that

very moment the wind blew.

The wind blew and it lifted him.

Suddenly he was being carried upwards on a cushion of air and he felt like he was a tiny leaf being blown away into a huge sky.

He felt lost.

But a moment later Steg's voice reached him, calling up from far below, encouraging him.

"You're doing great Dacky! Keep flying! Use your wings!"

Dacky did. He beat downwards. He felt himself lift. He tilted his wings and felt himself turn. He swooped down then looped up again.

Now he wasn't a leaf being blown away, now he was flying – he was a Pterosaur, he was a master of the air!

"Aaaak! Aaaak!"

Dacky knew what he had to do.

He flew straight across the city.

He soared above the streets, sailed across the green hill and swooped down between the tall buildings.

The tall glass tower came into sight. He

could see Marlin on the roof. The big man had hold of him and was dragging him in through a doorway. There was no time to think.

Dacky swooped.

******

"That's an end to your little game!" snarled Grubbler giving Marlin's arm a painful tug.

"Get off me!" Marlin shouted.

"Not a chance!" laughed Grubbler.

He had the door open now. He was holding it with his foot and pulling Marlin inside.

BANG!

The door slammed shut behind them and Marlin felt himself trapped.

"Got you now!" gloated Grubbler.

But in that very last moment, before the door had closed, Marlin thought he saw something swooping overhead and he thought he heard a cry.

"Aaak! Aaaak!"

Could it be?! No, it was impossible – the Pterosaur couldn't really fly…But a strange feeling of hope leapt up inside Marlin and that gave him strength.

He kicked Grubbler's shin very hard and pulled his arm free.

"Aargh!" Grubbler roared in fury and Marlin dived backwards through the door.

He fell onto the roof and tried to

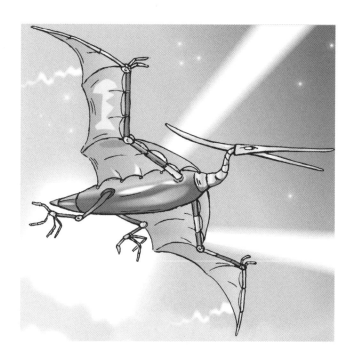

scramble away but Grubbler was straight
onto him, grabbing with his powerful arms.

Marlin was lifted – but now it was Dacky
who had hold of him, not Grubbler!

"Hold on boy!" the creature shouted.

His great wings beat down – once, twice
three times – and the force of the wind
knocked Grubbler off his feet.

Marlin and Dacky soared away and
the furious man stared after them, too
astonished even to speak.

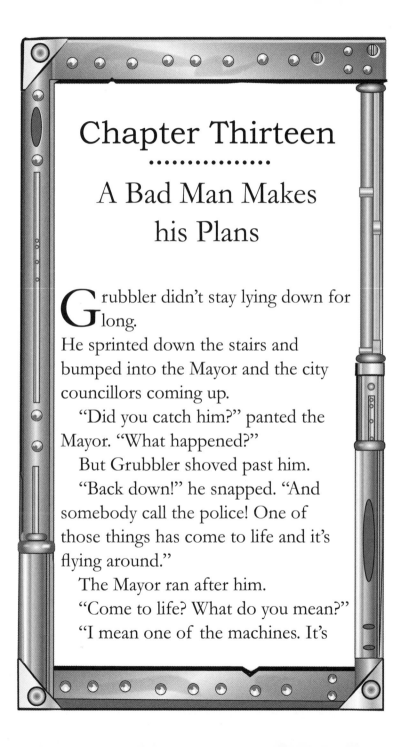

Chapter Thirteen

· · · · · · · · · · · · · · ·

A Bad Man Makes his Plans

Grubbler didn't stay lying down for long.

He sprinted down the stairs and bumped into the Mayor and the city councillors coming up.

"Did you catch him?" panted the Mayor. "What happened?"

But Grubbler shoved past him.

"Back down!" he snapped. "And somebody call the police! One of those things has come to life and it's flying around."

The Mayor ran after him.

"Come to life? What do you mean?"

"I mean one of the machines. It's

got out of the museum and it attacked me. You know what that means?"

The Mayor looked at him, confused.

"Well, I er…"

"It means that if one of the machines can escape, they all can!" snapped Grubbler.

He dived into the lift and pulled the Mayor in after him.

"We've got to bring the plan forward."

"Well yes, I suppose…do you think we should have another meeting?…"

But Grubbler ignored him. He was thinking hard.

"Listen," he snapped as the lift raced downwards towards the ground floor. "Here's what we'll do. I'll call Snickenbacker at once. He's got lots of people and lots of trucks. They can go straight to the museum and start pulling the monsters apart before it's too late."

"Oh yes, pull the monsters apart," agreed the Mayor. "We don't like monsters…"

PING!

The lift arrived and Grubbler stormed out.

Dacky landed on the grass close to where Flame was waiting with the Troodons. It wasn't the smoothest landing. Marlin went rolling over, clutching the precious battery to his chest.

Dacky sprawled on his front and his wings scraped along in the mud. But the crash landing didn't bother the Troodons.

"You can fly! You can fly!" they squeaked, running over to help him up.

"It's quite easy," shrugged Dacky. "Nothing to get excited about…"

But really he was very pleased with himself.

Flame looked down at Marlin.

"What happened?"

"I got it," nodded Marlin, holding up the battery. "But they nearly caught me. Dacky arrived just in time."

Flame turned to the others.

"Well done everyone!" he called. "But I don't think we should stay here too long…"

Even as he spoke, they heard voices shouting in the distance and the sound of a police siren came wailing across the city, getting louder.

"Dacky – can
you fly again?"
"Of course," sniffed
the Pterosaur.

"Then go! Fly straight
back to the museum and
take the battery."

"Certainly."

Dacky hopped over and
took the cylinder from
Marlin. As he did so
he lowered his great
beak.

"Well done
boy," he said.
"You were very brave."

Marlin grinned up at him.

"Goodbye!" called Dacky. Then he turned
into the wind, stretched his wings and was
gone.

"You too, little ones!" called Flame. "Run
as fast as you can, straight back the way we
came!"

The Troodons hopped over to Marlin.

"Well done boy," they both said. "You were very brave."

"Thank you," said Marlin.

Then they turned and darted away into the shadows with a laugh.

"Now us," smiled Flame.

And he picked Marlin up – gently this time – and lowered him onto his back. Marlin slipped down into the seat.

"Ready Marlin?"

"Ready Flame!"

And they were off.

Marlin leaned back and tried to catch sight of Dacky in the sky, but he was already gone. Now there were only stars, passing steadily by as they raced along.

"You did well," said Flame. "Tell me what happened up in the tower."

"They were having a meeting," began Marlin – and he told the T-Rex what he had discovered.

Flame grunted.

"Scrap metal, eh?"

"Yes! We've got to do something," Marlin replied. "Or they'll try to take you away."

"Don't worry," replied Flame. "I'm sure we'll be fine. Protos will be back with us soon and he'll know what to do."

And he sounded so certain that Marlin believed what he said and settled back in his seat. He yawned, suddenly exhausted from his adventure.

Yes, Protos was very wise. He would know what to do…

And then Marlin discovered that riding in a safe seat, high up on the back of a friendly T-Rex, is the perfect way to fall asleep.

******

Far away, in a very big house on the other side of the city, Howard H. Snickenbacker was also asleep – but at that moment he was woken by an urgent buzzing sound.

BUZZZ...BUZZZ…BUZZZ…

He sat up, grumbling, and fumbled for his phone.

"Yes? Who?!" he snapped. "Grubbler? This had better be important!"

It was pitch black in Snickenbacker's bedroom, far too dark to see – but if it had been a bit lighter, and if you had been able to see his face, you would certainly not have liked the greedy smile that was now slowly spreading across it.

It was the smile of a predator that not had a good meal for a long time and had just smelled something interesting.

"I see...yes I understand...well that shouldn't be a problem."

Snickenbacker snapped the phone off and slipped smoothly out of his bed, his expensive silk pyjamas hissing, snake-like, over the sheets.

He walked across the bedroom – it was very large, because he was very rich – to the window. And he reached out a hand to the curtains.

Below him, in the yard, his army was waiting.

It was an army of diggers and bulldozers and giant trucks covered with claws and hooks. They were all painted black, and looked like a colony of gigantic insects. Sleeping insects. But soon to be woken.

Snickenbacker picked up his phone again.

"Smith? It's me. Wake up the men – we're going hunting!"

How to find
secret dinosaurs
where you live

Mysterious tracks disappearing into the mist...
Find out more about clawprints on page 112.

Did a large creature get tangled in this wire fence?

How to find
Secret dinosaurs
where you live

It's usually easy to tell if there are Dinoteks living near you - just keep your eyes open for the clues.

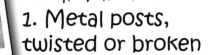

1. Metal posts, twisted or broken

Look out for unexplained damage to metal fences. Remember, it takes something very strong or incredibly heavy to twist metal out of shape like this.

Start a notebook and keep a record of anything you find.

111

How to find
Secret dinosaurs
where you live

2. Tracks & Clawprints

This enigmatic photo was taken early one morning. Two mysterious lines of prints could be seen leading away into the mist. They were like bird claw prints - only *much* bigger...

Some Dinoteks are so heavy they will sometimes even leave prints on roads and tarmac paths.

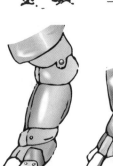

Stegosaurus

Centrosaurus

3. Signs of damage

Dinoteks are usually careful but sometimes tree branches get snapped.

This tree was probably already weak when an accidental bump finished it off...

The biggest of the Dinoteks are the Sauropods. These titans are not really suited to life in towns and will only venture out onto the streets if there's no other choice (so you'll be lucky to see one).

This fallen tree bark may be another example of accidental damage caused by a passing Dinotek Sauropod - even though they try to be careful.

4. Track a T-Rex!

Dinotek T-Rexs are very active so there's a good chance you'll see signs of Rex activity.

This metal tooth may have been knocked out in a battle. The rust shows it has been lying on the ground for quite a while.

Look out for pavings cracked by heavy impacts...

...just like the one that tripped Marlin up (see page 59)

Have fun
(and always hunt safely!)

Whenever you go searching for Dinoteks it's a good idea to go with friends. Keep to safe areas that you know and remember to ask an adult before you go. *And most of all - have fun!*

It looks very much as if a heavy creature has leaned against this fence.
The damage wasn't caused by an impact as there are no splinters or shattered pieces.

A Mystery

· · · · · · · · · · · · · · · ·

Where do the Dinoteks come from?

The Dinoteks were created many years ago by Professor Alfred Augustus Cogwell. That's what the dusty old sign on the wall said. But who _was_ the Professor?

Model Centrosaurus

Herbivore. Cretaceous period.
Made by
Professor Alfred Augustus Cogwell.

Nobody knows. Nobody remembers. Only one thing is certain: he worked at the museum once. But time has passed and everything there has changed (well most things

anyway).

But there may be an answer.

If you want to find a clue go down the road to the city library. Go into the right room and look on the right shelf and you might spot a cardboard box tied up with string. Inside is a collection of notebooks that once belonged in the museum – in fact they once belonged to the Professor.

So if you want to know where the Dinoteks came from these papers could tell you...

A page from Alfred Cogwell's diary, written when he was still a teenager. Was this the day that he first got his idea for building the Dinoteks? "Could it really be done?" he asked himself...

June 19th - last night I dreamed that I was building a dinosaur.

Could it really be done?

Most of the Dinoteks seem to be shown in this first drawing: a Stegosaurus, a Pterosaur, a small Therapod (Troodon?) and a half-built Centrosaurus. Did he also dream about making a T-Rex?

This page from the Notebooks shows an early design for a Centrosaurus.

This is a small therapod Dinotek but not a Troodon - it's labelled as a Dinotek Coelurosaur.

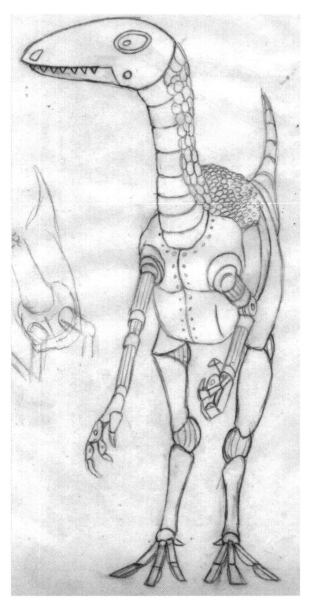

Detailed plans for a T-Rex claw.

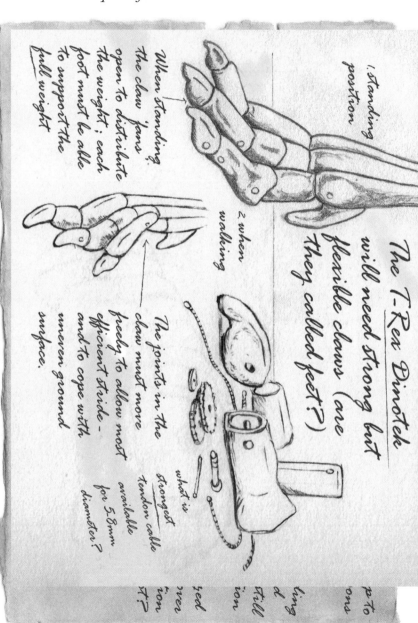

Designs for a Pterosaur claw showing how precisely it would be able to grip.

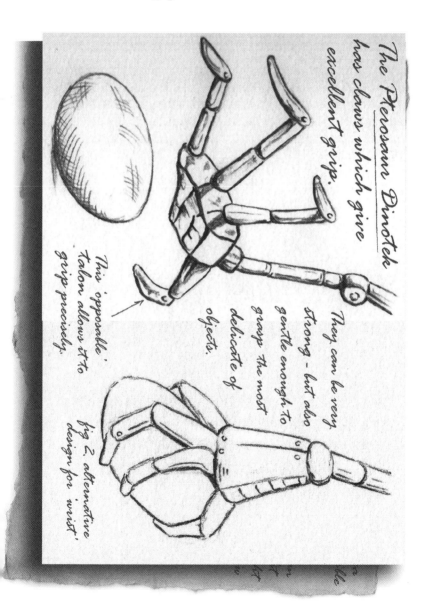

The Pterosaur Dinotek has claws which give excellent grip.

They can be very strong - but also gentle enough to grasp the most delicate of objects.

This 'opposable' talon allows it to grip precisely.

fig 2. alternative design for wrist.

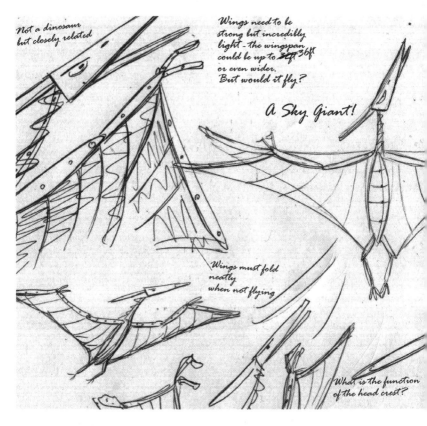

Not a dinosaur but closely related

Wings need to be strong but incredibly light - the wingspan could be up to ~~3ft~~ 36ft or even wider. But would it fly?

A Sky Giant!

Wings must fold neatly when not flying

What is the function of the head crest?

Pterosaurs were superbly adapted to life in the sky. Their large wings and excellent eyesight allowed them to search for food over great distances.
Professor Cogwell learned many lessons from nature in his own designs - but would the Dinotek Pterosaur actually fly, he wondered.

Imagine a museum with living machine dinosaurs

Above: a sketch of the museum entrance hall and (below) some designs for duck-billed Hadrosaurs

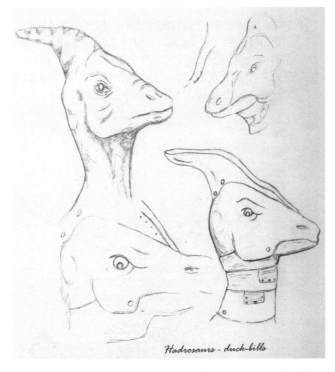

Hadrosaurs - duck-bills

About the author

N.S.Blackman has been writing and illustrating dinosaur stories since his early school days
in the Cretaceous era.

After emerging onto dry land he worked as a cleaner, a shop assistant, a teacher and a journalist before eventually evolving into his present form as a writer and illustrator.
His current habitat is London where he lives not far from Crystal Palace (where the world's oldest life-size dinosaur models also have their home).

If you have any questions about the Dinoteks or would like to send in your own designs and pictures to N.S.Blackman you can find him on Facebook or at www.dinoteks.com